Bimbofication of a Vigilante: Blackwing

The Silver Queen's Superharem, Volume 1

Layla Rose

Published by Comfy Cotton Underthings Publishing, 2022.

BIMBOFICATION OF A VIGILANTE: BLACKWING

First edition. March 5, 2022.

Copyright © 2022 Layla Rose.

ISBN: 979-8201070458

Written by Layla Rose.

Table of Contents

To the anonymous perverts whose suggestions guided Dixie's transformation and to the wonderful friends who support me and my weird, kinky writing.

Special thanks to WrenZephyr for the sexy, amazing cover art!

Prologue
The Restless Queen

Reality manipulation was too strong a power to leave in the hands of a villainess.

The Silver Queen's superpowers were so overpowered, all they left her with was a sense of boredom. She sat in her lavish estate, overlooking the world around her with mild disinterest. Worthless people went about their days, wholly unaware that they had been her slaves a year ago.

So many people acted like villains were looking for world domination. Not every bad guy had that in mind, but the Silver Queen gave it a shot. Heroes tried their best to stop her, but her ability to bend reality made it impossible for them to interfere. Everyone assumed the strongest power was a noble sense of justice. They were wrong; reality bending fucking rocked.

The world was The Silver Queen's and as she looked over the planet under her thrall, she felt... nothing. Dominating the whole world sounded like the ultimate power move, but in practice, it left a Monarch with little to do. What fun could you have with a world that said "How high?" every time she asked it to jump.

So The Silver Queen reset existence; not the whole thing, but everything that happened leading up to her planetary coup. Heroes and scientists tried to figure out where a sudden gap of missing time in the collective consciousness came from, and the woman responsible spent her time moping, trying to find new hobbies.

It was during this months-long moping session, digging into a tub of Neapolitan ice cream, that The Silver Queen was struck by a new idea. On the news, she noticed talk of a young heroine, one of The Bat's former proteges, making a name for herself. Much like her peers, she was multi-talented, highly independent, and driven by morals and justice and all the other bullshit heroes liked to say.

There was no saying what exactly made Dixie Grayson, Codename Blackwing, catch the Queen's eye, but the acrobatic ravenette gave her the idea she spent most of a year waiting for.

Vanquishing all the heroes and molding the whole world to suit her desires might have left The Silver Queen with nothing to hold her attention, but maybe the answer was smaller than that. She lived in a world of heroes and heroines; she could take her time with each one, toying with them from afar. Each one was a well of delicious possibilities, with bodies, minds, and backstories she could change at will.

Why dominate an entire world when you could take your time dominating its champions one by one?

And a plucky young gymnast would be her first unknowing plaything...

1
A Bigger Birdy

Breaking out on your own as a superhero was terrifying and exciting, like flying through the air without a safety net. Luckily, Dixie Grayson knew all about that. A gymnast in her youth and a vigilante sidekick through her teenage years, Dixie felt more at home leaping through the city skyline than she did with her feet on the ground.

Just because the life of a hero came naturally to her did not make it easy. Striking out on her own meant Blackwing was a hero people expected great things from. The whole city was her responsibility, which meant a lot of pressure and no margin for error. Every hero knew they could not stop every crime and save every person, but they were expected to try, and if that was not a great way to develop a stress migraine, nothing was.

Dixie knew all too well how important it was to spend some time living a street-level life. Maintaining her secret identity was important, but so was maintaining her mental health. Weeks of hardcore patrolling and brawling were finally wearing on the young heroine, so she needed to find a way to relax and let go of her burdens for a night before they drove her crazy.

Thankfully, unlike a certain cowled grump, she knew she had to take breaks occasionally to remind herself that she was a human in her twenties and allowed to act like it. She convinced Barbie, her bestie and on-again-off-again girlfriend, to come out with her to a house party. Barbie was still moonlighting as Batlass, one of The Bat's other sidekicks, so she could use the night off.

Pool parties were Dixie's go-to kind of party. She loved to swim, the drinks flowed freely, and she didn't mind the way Barbie looked at her toned body in a bikini.

Unfortunately, on their way to the party, something was off. She couldn't put her finger on it; she just felt a sense of vulnerability fluttering in her chest. She almost told Barbie to turn around to settle for a night in.

Still, she *desperately* needed a night free from responsibility, and her old college friends were dragging her out to give her just that. Dixie Grayson had a reputation as the life of any party, so she would be there mingling and trying not to make Barbie feel jealous. She wasn't the only one who had their eyes on her perky chest holstered in that cute striped bikini.

Except it was odd. As the night went on, the band of that bikini top felt snug across her back. Maybe it was a tighter fit than she thought. That was her justification, at least until she realized the cups were ill-fitting, too. That was unexpected, because she remembered the whole ensemble fitting like a glove in the dressing room when she made the pre-summer impulse purchase.

Barbie clearly noticed. Hell, everyone at the pool was noticing. "Hey, babe? Is that a push-up top or something? You're looking kind of... mashed in there."

Was that a result of the water? Some swelling from lingering in the shallow end of the pool all night? "It isn't. I've been feeling weird all night. Cover for me?" Too curious to ignore this unexpected chesty development, Dixie slipped off to the washroom.

When she looked in the mirror, she could no longer blame the tightness on a little water. Suddenly, all the extra attention she was getting tonight made sense.

The cups that securely held her in earlier in the night suddenly looked overwhelmed. Dixie's chest was modest in comparison to some of the other heroines in her contact list, but the Dixie in the mirror was poking out everywhere; cleavage, side boob, underboob.

Her tits were undeniably bigger than when she left the apartment. Heck, they were bigger than when she got out of the pool! Dixie had enough experience dating women with figures across the spectrum to guess she was looking at more than a D cup.

And the tingling still wasn't going away. They were still getting bigger! At this rate, her bikini top was going to strangle her or tear itself apart against her.

Begrudgingly, she untangled herself from the garment and letting full breasts drop free. She watched in the mirror, perplexed, as minutes passed and her chest finally settled to what she guessed might be an E or F cup, with pronounced, erect nipples to match their new heft.

Dixie groaned, wondering if this was the work of some crafty villain or one of her magically inclined friends pulling a prank on her. She did intervene with a museum heist recently, so maybe she accidentally touched some kind of cursed idol? That sounded like her luck.

All she knew was she officially had a bikini too small to hold what her annoying adopted brother Jay would later call her 'big bazongas.'

Sitting on the counter next to the sink, Dixie pulled out her phone, taking a photo of herself In this topless, boobified state. Her arms smushed her swollen breasts together when she held the device in front of her with both hands. That was a new sensation, letting her know that these "upgraded" breasts were even more sensitive than before.

She texted Barbie, "Do you think anyone have a really big bikini or a very loose shirt to spare?" She attached the photo for evidence. She might have been the life of the party, but she had to get back to her apartment before she became the center of attention for a much harder to explain reason.

She got her reply quick. "I'll ask around. Also, I'm saving that." Well, at least Barbie appreciated the new look. That was a small silver lining.

2
Costume Change

Blackwing watched from a rooftop, overlooking Bloodholme, the city she adopted as her own to protect. It was a rare quiet night in the crime-ridden city. It was also chilly for early September, but her suit was designed to keep her safe and keep her warm.

Her expanded chest, which she still could not adequately explain, was mashed into a sports bra under her padded armor, but at least she was protected and her body could tune out the cold. Her red cheeks, on the other hand, were making her wish she had taken after The Bat and incorporated a cowl into her outfit.

"Getting a little nippy out?" Barbara's voice was in her ear; the redhead was on comms for the night, which meant she was comfy and warm watching monitors and passing along intel.

"Don't say it like that. I'm still sensitive about that," Blackwing joked.

Dixie could almost hear Barbie smirking over her earpiece. "I know."

The cheeky tease would have earned an equally suggestive reply, but a set of eyes from a nearby balcony spotted her, cutting play time short. Dixie sized up the onlooker, but she wasn't threatened. She saw no weapons, and it was not like people did not know Blackwing was around.

When a city ended up with its own live-in vigilante, word got around fast. People going about their lives grew accustomed to noticing a figure swinging through the air, framed by gray clouds. She would grapple away to a new rooftop and her appearance would be an interesting footnote that guy would share with his friends later.

This sighting wouldn't be quite that standard. Before the vigilante could pull out her grappling gun, a chill ran up her back. It was a tingling, unexplainable feeling oddly reminiscent of the way her chest felt the night of the pool party a week earlier.

The next chill was easier to explain. Looking down, dumbfounded, Dixie watched as the pants of her suit seemingly dissolved, the durable weave unweaving into nothingness. Her boots crept higher up her calf to compensate, but not much. Instead, she watched practical fabric replaced by the transparency of fishnet stockings.

The padded, combat-tested material of her outfit, normally designed to protect her from the odd knife or low-caliber firearm, thinned out into a clingy material. In the same way her legs were left all but bare, her sleeves dematerialized up her arms until only her upper body was covered, if you could call it that.

The night wind cut through the fabric like it was not there, making it clear to Dixie and her cold nipples trying to pierce through her costume, that her sports bra had vanished, too.

Her arms and legs, beyond the boots and fishnets, were completely exposed. The fabric of her tight leotard was not generous enough to cover the bottoms of Dixie's ass. Normally, she was proud of her bubble butt, but not enough to let them peek out in public! Now, she was stuck with two sets of chilled cheeks to deal with.

Looking around in confusion, then back at the observer on the balcony, Dixie was perplexed. The man on his balcony was gawking, realizing his interesting footnote just became a full-blown story none of his friends would believe.

Blackwing shivered, knowing she could not fight crime like this tonight. "Hey, Batlass? Do you have eyes on me?"

"Oh. They're on you. Getting Sparrow to cover for you. Mighty Girl would be proud."

"At least Mighty Girl is bulletproof. And coldproof," she grumbled. She was not looking forward to the trip home.

3
Read My New Lips

Dixie woke up annoyed. Fighting crime was harder when her whole wardrobe consisted solely of leotards overnight. Unfortunately, crime did not take days off, even while the heroine waited for her new equipment order to be fulfilled. Blackwing still went out to bust up a meeting between the crime families of Bloodholme the night before, which thankfully took place indoors in a warm casino back room.

She busted up thugs on both ends, nimbly dodging attacks and being conscious of guns in her new gear, but an asshole of a crime boss and his shitty comment stuck with her all night.

"Did they send a crime-fighting stripper? Maybe you should put them fists down and put that pretty mouth to work," the Boss taunted. As he fled. Like a *coward*.

Sure, she did not expect much from crime lords, but it was rude regardless! It bugged her, particularly as the rumor mill was abuzz with stories of why Bloodholme's protector was suddenly stacked and dressed down, but she had to get out of her own head. Why was some jerk's meaningless comment sticking with her?

Rolling out of bed, she sighed. "Fucking ath'ole."

Dixie's blue eyes went wide, because the words felt and sounded wrong coming off her lips.

Her lips.

She scrambled to her feet and got to her vanity mirror. She remembered cleaning off her makeup the night before, but her lips had a soft, pink sheen like someone applied gloss to them in her sleep. They were glistening, and rubbing them with the back of her hand did nothing to change that.

The shimmer was not the only change to her mouth. Dixie's lips were at least twice as full as she remembered! Try as she might, she had pouty pillows like she was injected with lip fillers in her sleep or something. Panicking, she checked the feeds from her security cameras on her phone, but no one came in for some late-night glamourwork.

Dixie spoke a few words out loud, but she was not used to speaking around the puffy pink lips she now sported. Dealing with another mysterious change from the universe she had no answers for, Dixie tossed herself back on the bed and pulled out her phone. Before she would message anyone, she looked at herself one more time in the camera.

She was gonna hunt that bastard down. Part of her doubted he had something to do with the changes her body was going through, but either way, she was going to have words for him.

Unfortunately, those words would come out with a lisp.

4
50 Shades Lighter

Dixie was begrudgingly taking some time away from patrol. She had worked hard to adjust her acrobatics to compensate for the additional pounds of chest she was working with, but it was still best to play things safe while Barbie dug for answers to her situation. Dixie also had to replace her uniforms, which were all still skimpy leotards more suited for a stripper pole than a rooftop.

In fact, a lot of her wardrobe seemed to be comprised of leotards now. She didn't want to admit it, but Dixie felt the pleasing thrill of her swelling confidence when she put one of her skintight ensembles on. Barbie wasn't complaining, either. With her new big naturals and kissable lips, the redhead was very handsy these days. They weren't exclusive, but they were definitely back in the "on-again" stage of their relationship.

Still, just because she loved them as a fashion choice did not make them suitable for crime-fighting sprees.

As far as silver linings went, Dixie was glad to know she was getting better at talking with her absurdly puffy lips. The lisp was minimal now, but she was still not sure who or what was doing this to her. Zee promised she was not charming her ex-girlfriend into some strip club fantasy, and an inventory of the museum confirmed nothing she touched there should have had any lingering effects. The universe was making subtle and not so subtle changes to her, and Dixie was just along for the ride.

It was also not over. After waking up next to Zee in the morning, (because Barbie wasn't the only one who could appreciate the more gropable Grayson,) the magician asked Dixie if she had highlighted her hair before they went to the bar the night before. She had not.

"And you didn't feel anything magical last night?"

"Oh, it was pretty magical, alr—"

"Zee, focus." Dixie needed her paramours to get a *little* less horny about her predicament.

Zee scrunched her nose. "Right. Sorry. No spells. This isn't magic, which means I can't undo it."

Dixie groaned, resigned to monitoring the situation. As expected, her black hair was a chocolate brown in the morning, honey brown by lunch, and as the evening set with Dixie alone in her apartment staring at the reflection in her mirror, she could barely believe she was the one staring back at her.

Dixie Grayson was a full-on platinum blonde; not a dark root to be seen.

The transforming young woman squirmed in frustration. She had no answers and with each change, she was getting more exhausted by the fruitless search. New boobs, new lips, new hair. Part of Dixie was starting to wonder if she should just give in and see where this odd cosmic transformation took her.

5
Hanging Up Her Spandex

Complacent was a word Dixie never wanted to describe herself, but she was raised by The Bat to be practical The genius gymnast was not afraid of a little work, and she was learning to move more gracefully, regardless of the unexpected changes to her body. Unfortunately, there was a nagging realization sitting in the back of her mind and, eventually, Dixie had to accept it as fact: Blackwing, for the foreseeable future, had to be done.

Zee and the rest of Dixie's mystic friends were still researching possible answers, and Barbie was using her genius brain to track down leads, but two months of searching came up with zero results. Dixie accepted that things about her might keep changing.

It would not take a genius-level intellect for people to notice that Blackwing and Dixie Grayson were going through the same changes. The heroine with the sudden massive breasts, blonde hair, and pillow lips and the heiress who looked like she was fast-tracking her way through a rebellious transformation were too clearly the same woman. Questions were being asked about both her identities, and she knew all too well how important her secret identity was as a vigilante without superpowers.

With a sigh, Dixie accepted her call to an early, and hopefully temporary retirement. It was time to return to civilian life. Maybe they would find answers and the Blackwing of old would return, but the practical ex-vigilante would spend the present focusing on what she would do with her life out of costume.

The Silver Queen never failed to impress herself. Sure, she may have been heavy-handed with some physical changes, but all it took was a kernel of doubt to fuel Blackwing's natural pragmatism. Weeks went by and the media asked where the clearly troubled Blackwing might have disappeared to, confirming the Queen's success.

Now that Blackwing, the vigilante, was no more, The Silver Queen mused on how much more fun she could have with Dixie Grayson, the woman.

6
Impulsive, Reckless, Sexy

Dixie slammed her empty shot glass on the bar top to the cheers of her friends. Another night out in the Bloodholme nightlife and Dixie had all eyes on her. Initially, Dixie was partying to cope with the loss of her vigilante life, and her family was rightfully worried about her.

Eventually, the anger and loss turned to acceptance. Dixie was still learning to live with all the free time that came with being a civilian, but she could get used to this becoming her new normal.

Being a party girl was always an aspect of Dixie's cover when she needed a secret identity. Now that the "mundane" parts of her life were all she had, Dixie decided she would take some time embracing the lifestyle she played at for years. Barbie came out with her on some of her off nights, but the bookish nerd was more of an introvert. She was also working harder as Batlass to deal with the loss of Blackwing in Bloodholme.

That was fine. Barbie wasn't the only person she could spend her nights with. The occasional nights out were quickly becoming a near nightly activity.

Late nights, heavy drinking, and grinding on bodies on the dance floor. The men, women, and nonbinary baddies of her city were openly feeling her up out there, and she could finally let herself enjoy it. The Dixie she pretended to be was a party girl, but the more she embraced that side of her, the more fun the ex-vigilante had as a hedonist.

Could she be doing more with her time? Sure; she was brilliant and she knew it, but did she really need to right away? Dixie had given so much of her life to improving the world as Blackwing, and now she could take a few weeks or months to enjoy the life of luxury her adopted father handed to her. She would pick a path to follow eventually. Until she was ready to settle down, there were other clever people in the world to pick up her slack.

Dixie went from being the life of the party to the queen of the nightlife. She was living in the moment, hopping from bar to bar and taking wild adventures skinny dipping in Sun City or gambling away thousands of dollars from her trust fund in Vegas.

There was a daring suggestion from one of the guys she was all over at tonight's club, and it struck her as so bold, before she knew it, Dixie and her entourage found a late-night tattoo parlor and threw her in a chair with her pants off.

She slept in late the next morning. She never used to sleep in late, even with her crime-fighting extracurriculars. Now that she could do it after every night of reckless celebration, she was growing to appreciate how refreshing it was to wake up on her own schedule.

While she slept, Dixie's phone was abuzz with men and women from the club excited to see the final result of her impulse tattoo. It was so unlike her! At least, it was so unlike the old her, but maybe Dixie was allowed to be someone different in this new chapter of her life. She had some missed texts from Barbie, just checking in on her and reminding her to drink some water. Dixie would find time to hang out with her when her eyes adjusted to the daylight.

Sneaking away from last night's snoring conquest, Dixie slipped into the washroom, pulled her panties on to retain *some* sense of modesty, and took a picture of the inside of her left thigh, just below her entrance. Inscribed in fresh ink were the words, *"For Your Mischief and Misuse."*

Besides the party partners on her list of Snapchat favorites, it was the kind of cheeky message hidden away for the lucky few to find at the end of a very good night.

Okay, maybe at the rate she was going, the lucky few dozen, but that still made her new tattoo an exclusive treat for those who ended their nights out gaining entrance to something slightly more exclusive than the VIP Room of the Icebank Lounge.

7
The New Normal

The Silver Queen left Dixie to her own devices, watching with intent interest as she became the popular party girl she always could have been. Maybe who she always *should* have been. The villainess knew the idea was right the moment it clicked in her head. She had been debating the next change to shake things up for Dixie; why not cut right to the source?

Months passed of Dixie settling into non-hero life, making her mark on every club, dive, and house party of note on either coast. Life was gaining a sense of normalcy, which was not the kind of thing Dixie ever said about her life. From her tragic origins to her whirlwind adoption by a cowled vigilante, odd and unexpected were Dixie's normal.

With her Blackwing leotard retired, Dixie decided to be content living life not as who she was then, but instead, who she was in the moment. Her permanent dye job was ages in the past in her eyes, so she finally had the time to accept and even embrace her new look, mysterious transformations and all.

Her stacked chest paired with her fit body got everyone's attention wherever she went. Once she had that attention, Dixie noticed and savored how people could not stop watching her lips hungrily with every word she spoke.

As for the hair, she could hardly remember a life where she would look in the mirror and see jet black locks framing her face. Something about seeing herself as a blonde just made sense.

And... why wouldn't it? It always worked, right? Dixie stared at her reflection, recognizing herself. Her memory was foggy, she assumed because another late night of drinking was catching up to her, but the more she inspected the elements of her face, the clearer the picture of her past became.

It was her face. Her body. Ever since she went through puberty, she remembered the way everyone started treating her differently. The gifted gymnast blossomed in a big way, and suddenly, her growing chest was all anyone could see when they weren't following her lips. She could reliably tease anyone for failing to maintain eye contact as their gaze darted down into her impressive cleavage or the eager nipples constantly poking through her tops. People would lose track of what they were saying mid-sentence if she licked her lips. It was a social superpower she grew addicted to as she got older.

And she clearly wasn't the only addict to the benefits of her bombshell body. A pair of freckled arms wrapped around her from behind, giving her massive tits a squeeze. Barbie entered the bathroom, having put on panties since their afternoon booty call, but not much else.

Dixie could feel the warmth of her kinda sorta girlfriend's perky chest against her back. She couldn't remember the last time her and Barbie were the same size. "Mmm, careful. Get too handsy and you're going to be late for your patrol," she murmured, still in a daze of recollection.

Dixie was happy to fight crime with her adopted family, first as Bluejay, then as Blackwing, but her time as a heroine was limited. Dixie was not superpowered like some of her peers, and as she developed, she grew out of her nimble acrobat's figure.

As an adult, attention became the norm, and as her siblings and even Barbie stopped taking her seriously, Dixie spent more time living on the party girl side of her double life.

Eventually, shortly after starting college, she decided to bring her career in vigilantism to an end prematurely. It was a good run, and sometimes she even missed it, but Dixie Grayson was not built to save the world, physically or mentally, and she had not been for a long time.

"Maybe I should have taken an early retirement, too. I would have had more time for this," Barbie joked, kissing Dixie's neck. It was just playful banter; Barbie loved her life as Batlass too much to quit. The difference in their lifestyles was what kept them from committing to their relationship fully.

Why was she reminiscing about the adventures of her youth? A time when she expected life to lead her in a much different direction. Was she regretting her choices?

Dixie's glazed blue eyes came back into focus. Two fingers trailed down Dixie's hips, nudging the inside of her thighs to part so Barbie could tease Dixie's slit, shaking her out of the odd bout of nostalgia. What was there to regret again?

"I can call The Bat right now and tell him you quit if you can just never stop doing that," she said with a sigh, wavering when Barbie's digits entered her. What was there to regret again?

Dixie looked at herself in the mirror one last time. "Hey? Do you think I could pull off dark hair?"

Barbie looked up from the back shoulder where she was planting kisses. "Honestly? I can't imagine you as anything but my sexy blonde," she whispered in Dixie's ear. Yeah. Barbie was going to be running late.

The ex-vigilante was just a laid-back blonde bombshell whose idea of being "adventurous" had nothing to do with smoke bombs and grappling hooks. That was her life, and she was happy with what she had made of it. What else would she expect?

8
Insatiable

It was a typical night for Dixie. She may have stopped being The Bat's sidekick years ago, but Bryce still accepted her as his daughter. And he was a multi-billionaire. Having that kind of money let you become a gadget-wielding superhero with an arsenal of private military-grade vehicles.

It also meant you had the kind of money to set your adopted children up with the kind of trust funds that meant they never *had* to work.

Dixie was sure at some point in her life, she would want something to fill her time with beyond sex and alcohol. Nowadays, it was hard to imagine hating this life of promiscuous leisure.

All she had to concern herself with tonight was picking her next dance partner. There was a redhead hanging close to her, Lizzy, who desperately wanted Dixie's attention. People accused her of having a type, namely redheads, but her type was just hot people. Redheads were often just crazy hot.

With legs like hers, Lizzy certainly fit the bill.

Dixie had a reputation as a flirt at the bar, but tonight, something thrumming in her core was calling her out to the dance floor. When she realized the leggy redhead had caught Dixie eyeing her up and down, drinking her in and missing half of what she was saying,

Dixie gave into the call. She grabbed her new friend by the hand. "Sorry, just... do you want to dance?" Dixie was leading them out to the dance floor before she got an answer.

Dancing was one of Dixie's favorite hobbies, but now it was like a drive. She moved with the music, eliminating any inch of space between her and Lizzy. She was not thinking; she was only sensing. She felt the heat of the body in front of her and the friction as they pressed and writhed against one another. She could smell the sweat and perfume mingling on a freckled neck as she pulled in close.

"D-Dixie," a squeaked voice cautioned, but the blonde barely heard it as her fingers rode up the redhead's lean, supple thighs. Dixie grinned devilishly, hungrily as they made eye contact and she felt more space open up to her as Lizzy set her dancing stance slightly wider.

In the moment, surrounded by hot bodies, Dixie could not think to care if anyone noticed her hiking up her redhead's dress. Slipping into her panties. No thinking, just senses. Feelings, like the hot, wet folds enveloping Dixie's fingers as they slipped past Lizzy's defenses. As fast as they hit the dance floor, Dixie dragged an all-too-willing Lizzy to a coat room so she could taste her.

Dixie found her place between Lizzy's freckled thighs, burying her face and fingers into a needy, sopping cunt. The more Lizzy gave her, the more Dixie hungered for the redhead. Not just her; she could still feel the heat of the bodies she left on the dance floor. In the moment, her tongue was wholly devoted to toying with Lizzy's clit, but the night still had so much to offer. The dancefloor had so many tantalizing bodies she could fit in the spacious bed back in her loft.

Dixie stirred, tangled in her sheets, damp with sweat. There was a body she was tangled with as well, she realized as she kissed a spot between bare shoulder blades curly red hair. "Mmm, morning, Lizzy," she muttered.

"Ye sure know how tae make a girl feel special," a sheepish, notably accented voice teased. "Rebecca," the voice corrected, more amused than upset as she sat up in the bed.

Right. It had been a blur of a weekend. Dixie remembered bringing home Becca from the bar, but that was Friday night. Dawn was breaking on Monday and Rebecca, along with her dark-haired friend Annie nestled behind Dixie, were her newest conquests. As the fog of morning cleared from her sex-addled mind, Dixie remembered the women were, in fact, her bartenders from the night before.

They had sex three times between the bar closing and the morning, and even as she watched Rebecca collect her scattered garments, she felt the pull for one more fuck after a weekend of constant fucking. Rebecca saw the look of hunger she must have been intimately familiar with now, and while they both finally left to get some actual, uninterrupted sleep, she teasingly left Dixie with a word that stuck with her.

"Insatiable."

She felt insatiable. When she could see bodies moving and feel their heat and all the potential they offered, a drive built in Dixie she struggled to ignore. During the night, they almost got to sleep when Annie brushed up against Dixie's breast, and that small touch was enough to build back into their third and final fling.

After the girls left, Dixie managed three hours of sleep before waking up horny. She played with herself in the bed, then in the shower, even calling on the help of her favorite toy to feed her needs, frantically pumping the vibrating shaft deep into her until she came three times.

It changed nothing; by late afternoon, she was plagued with lewd thoughts about the people at the grocery store, making it hard to give a shit about which onions she needed for dinner. Dixie was always flirtatious, but something about all this free time and partying had pushed her into full-on nymphomania. Sex was becoming a distraction from the most basic non-sexual parts of her life.

She went to a club or bar each night that week. It did not matter if things were slower on weekdays and Dixie could not wait to take people home to have her fun. Dancing led to fucking a tattooed woman in the washroom and shots led to a guy with a flawless olive complexion railing her in the alley. And of course, she never went home alone by the end of the night.

She didn't call Barbie when she was in heat like this. When things were bad, names and faces blurred in her mind, their importance paling in comparison to her need to feed a lust she could not fully satisfy. And if she called Barbie by another hot redhead's name, their casual situationship would come to an abrupt end.

9
All Eyes on Dixie

Dixie was no stranger to VIP rooms and special tables. Her name was hot on the lips of every socialite and paparazzi worth a damn, so if she did not book a room for herself, an invitation to join someone's VIP party would find her shortly upon her arrival.

There were a dozen people in tonight's VIP section, all invited by the richest man in the room. According to the attractive older woman Dixie was doing her best to talk to, he was a crime boss or something. Barbie and her family would disapprove. In another life, maybe Dixie would have agreed with them.

But the nightlife brought together all kinds, and it wasn't Dixie's place to judge. If he was really such a bad guy, The Bat would deal with him. Dixie just had to keep herself safe and enjoy her night.

The host kept sneaking lusty glances at Dixie, but the stunning silver-haired woman on his arm was the one unabashedly undressing Dixie with her eyes. Talking to a sexy cougar was already stirring Dixie's blood, but that look of craving had Dixie's entire body on fire. Nowhere was she burning harder than between her legs.

Everyone was laughing and drinking until the milf of a woman noticed Dixie squirming and biting her lip. The more Dixie's need built, the harder it was to hide it. It was hard to believe she kept a secret identity once upon a time. "Are you doing okay, sugar?"

The crime boss' girlfriend saw the way Dixie shifted in her seat and met her eyes. Something about her made Dixie's stomach flutter, adding to the overwhelming sensations she was dealing with. "Need to move a little? Sounds like you should dance for us," the silver-haired goddess suggested knowingly.

"Yeah?" Dixie asked, her thoughts foggy as she trying to keep herself under control.

"Absolutely. We saw you dancing out on the floor. I'm sure we'd all love to see more of you," she said, her words laced with seductive intent that shot down to Dixie's center. "Right, baby?" The head of the table smirked and nodded, gesturing to the center of the VIP room and the laughing and conversation stopped.

Taking a deep breath, Dixie stepped to the center of the room. All five sets of eyes watched the blonde bombshell, flooding her with adrenaline and dopamine. She started moving to the music thumping through the club, acutely aware of each pair of eyes watching her hips sway or her tits bounced to the music.

The heat rose in her, pushing her. Dixie endured weeks of lust driving her mad, but tonight was different. It was the eyes. Knowing everyone's attention was not just on her, but her body. Dixie craved it as much as she desired for every person in that VIP room to fuck her.

Maybe they would, but for now, she wanted to show more. Dixie pulled her dress over her head as she danced. Each new square inch of her laid bare for thirsty eyes to drink in heightened the thrill. She could feel her horny need dripping down the inside of her thigh, glistening for the room to see, and she did not care.

She had no clue when this taste for exhibitionism developed, but it hit her hard tonight as everyone watched her undo her bra, leaving her massive tits restrained by nothing but the arm she wrapped around them.

The air in the room was thick with anticipation, and that anticipation echoed through Dixie's body. When she released her perfect breasts, letting them dance and bounce to the beat, Dixie shuddered as she came, hit by the orgasm she realized she had been building to since taking her makeshift stage.

Having a room of people locked on her naked body, fantasizing about fucking her was a rush Dixie now understood was on par with *actually* getting fucked. She wanted people to look at her like that again.

She *needed* it.

10
Another Costume to Strip Away

"Come on, Tweety. You're up next," a bubbly dancer whispered in Dixie's ear.

Dixie shrugged, standing from a patron's lap. "I'm sorry, sir, but duty calls. Maybe when I'm done you can keep letting me talk you into a more private dance," she teased, the very thought of it sending a jolt to her center. She had to be careful; it was early in the night, and she could not soak through a pair of panties before her first dance.

The patron was not just a patron, he was a crime boss. He was *the* crime boss. More importantly for Dixie, he was the owner of the club employing her.

After her impromptu audition in his VIP room, the Boss' silver-haired date suggested she could find a very fulfilling career with one of his many business ventures. Understanding the intoxicating satisfaction she derived from putting her body on display and dancing for others to admire, Dixie jumped at the chance to become one of the Boss' new dancers.

After a week of learning the ropes as the Midnight Alibi Club's newest stripper, she wanted to make it clear to him how much she appreciated her job.

But first, she had a pole waiting for her.

After touching up her makeup and changing, Tweety waited for her name to be called by the DJ. Her chosen song started playing and the dancer made her way onto the stage, dressed for the night's theme.

She had been excited about tonight, because the boss declared it "Superho Night," which meant Dixie got to dress up like a hero or a villain. In a city like Bloodholme, the epicenter of costumed crime and crime fighters, the crowd ate the theme up. Everyone, from your law-abiding citizens to your two-bit thugs, fantasized about seeing naughty superheroines giving into their base urges to strip down for them.

If only they knew one of their entertainers for the evening was a genuine former member of the hero game doing just that. The tips would be *insane*.

Dixie considered dressing up as a slutty parody of The Bat. He would hate that if he ever found out, but the boss suggested a villainous costume instead. Dixie loved the red corset and fishnets decorated with card suits as an homage to Jester.

The Bat might hate her dressing up as the ditzy villain more, but Dixie was an adult who made her own choices. Well, technically, she was letting the Boss make her choices. Regardless, she loved her new look and the way the corset was designed to strip away easily.

The moment Dixie's stripper heels stepped onto the stage, she was immediately hit with the heightened feeling of a room of eyes watching her as she strutted up toward the pole. She felt their eyes on the ass poking out from a skirt that might as well have been a belt. She felt their eyes on her luscious lips when she licked them. Most obviously, she felt their eyes as they watched her tits, spilling out of the top of her corset, as they bounced with her movements.

With her background in gymnastics, Dixie took to the pole like a natural. The way she moved, it was like she had danced around this pole hundreds of times.

And... she had. As she draped herself upside down, her legs wrapped around the spinning pole, reality spun with her. Dixie had lost her gift for crime-fighting before she started college, but she traded it in for a new gift. Her first dance was not a week ago; it was *years* ago.

One of Dixie's freshman roommates had started a job at the club, intending to earn cash while she earned her degree. Dixie was not pressed for money, but her curiosity got the better of her. She tagged along for a night and fell in love with everything. The club, the lighting, the gorgeous women, the blaring music, and the way the crowd watched her.

Exhibitionism was not some new kink for Dixie; this was who she was. She found her true identity on that stage, peeling off clothes for money and, far more importantly, the lust of her audience. Barbie objected to her lover joining her new line of work, worried she was leaning too hard into objectifying herself. Dixie couldn't care less about letting people treat her like a sex object; that was just second nature to her.

She could have stopped dancing after college. She had opportunities and a host of other talents, but dancing and putting herself on display came as natural to her as breathing. She loved the stage. She loved the pole. She loved every handsy, grindy lapdance.

Barbie could save the lives of the citizens of Bloodholme, but Tweety gave them fuckable fantasies that made life worth living.

And getting off to it multiple times a night, of course.

11
Not the Brightest Birdy Anymore

Everyone said bending reality was dangerous and rewriting the past had dangerous repercussions that could shake the very foundations of the space-time continuum.

Those people were *fucking lame.* That, or they never experienced the joys of holding a heroine's life in their hands, tugging at the strands of fate that made up her past, and unravelling them to remake her as something more entertaining. The Silver Queen should make more changes for Dixie to deal with in the present day, but the Queen could not resist tampering with Dixie's formative experiences at least one more time.

And so, she created one more ripple in Dixie's past to watch the repercussions.

Despite not being a vigilante like her other adopted siblings, Dixie still received messages reaching out to check on her, given the dangerous elements they all knew frequented her strip club.

They all silently knew she could be doing more with her life, putting her quick wit and degrees to better use, but none of them judged her for wanting to live a simple, happy life. Heroing was busy work, so drop-ins were less common, but she was still a loved member of the family and her call history illustrated that.

Dixie was lounging on her couch and texting with Scarlet Sparrow, who was in college himself these days. She could not imagine balancing a full course load on top of patrols and missions. When they talked about their lives, it sounded overwhelming. Balancing dancing with her studies had been enough to push Dixie past whelmed at points, so when Tom asked if he could borrow her old bio-chem textbooks and notes, Dixie wanted to be helpful and ease his burdens any way she could. She skipped off to her study.

Except... well, it was the darnedest thing. Where did she leave her old schoolbooks again? She could have sworn they were on her bookshelf. She had worked hard and spent a pretty penny amassing heavy hardcovers and ring binders of her knowledge, so when she bought her apartment, had she not brought the fruits of her studies?

Maybe she just imagined the hours carefully unpacking the evidence of her learnedness from a heavy trunk, arranging them by subject on her shelves. It made more sense that she was misremembering. She had a knack for forgetting things. That was one rare thing she was confident to be true.

Accepting that truth, college formed more clearly in her head. She was constantly forgetting her books and missing deadlines. It was hard to pass classes when you were unabashedly absentminded.

She always struggled in school; no one expected an airhead like her to stay on top of her studies, and her notoriously high libido all but doomed her. Dixie's head might have been empty of college-level science and math she ignored, but she had vivid memories of waking up still dripping with cum after every house party. She even capped off Sorority Rush Week by instigating an all-night orgy she was sure the girls of Omega Mu Gamma remembered long after Dixie dropped out.

And she did drop out. Dixie accepted that college was just... well, it was harder than she expected. She was an average student at best in high school, but college-level lessons just went over her head. She couldn't understand how geniuses like Tom and Barbie did it.

Dixie took her failure in stride, long ago accepting she was the one dummy in a family of prodigies.

In the end, she just wasn't college material. She had a great job dancing already, so why waste time failing Freshman Bio a second time?

Returning from a blank-stared zone out, Dixie looked back at her text messages and snorted.

"You goober! What would a brainiac like you need with my textbooks anyway?"

Given the super smart shit Tom was probably studying for whatever Honors program he got accepted into, Dixie guessed he was just teasing her with a request like that. Her siblings poked fun at her, not to be malicious, but because sometimes it took her a minute to realize the joke and they could all have a good laugh at another dumb blonde moment from Dixie. Barbie scolded them, but she was usually still chuckling at her lover's expense.

Rolling her eyes, Dixie looked back at her shelves, lined wall to wall with Blu-rays and video games. Because that's what those shelves were always for. Her adopted father suggested the room could be a study when she moved in, but Dixie dismissed that idea with a giggle. A media room would be much more useful; she got her fill of reading in high school, and a movie was easier to watch when her hands were occupied.

12
A Kept Woman

Dixie loved her job as a dancer. She wouldn't trade it for anything else because what other job would let her strip naked—or okay, *close* to naked—for dozens of people and grind up against customers in private rooms? (There were rules about how much customers could touch the girls, but Boss made sure the bouncers knew Dixie had special permission to let people touch her as much as they wanted.) Without a college degree, this was the only job Dixie had experience with, and she made good money.

But... well, Dixie grew up as a rich man's daughter. That came with expensive tastes and experience being taken care of and spoiled.

The money Dixie made stripping was quickly consumed by her spending habits, and with her flighty memory, she was terrible at keeping a budget. She was an impulsive spirit, and while she loved that about herself, her wallet did not.

Sure, she could always ask her adopted father for money or more access to her trust, but these days, he seemed wary of what she might do if he let her have too much. He was also living a super important life being The Bat, so Dixie did not want to bother him when she didn't have to.

It was lucky for Dixie that Bryce was not the only strong, rich man in her life. The owner of the club had taken quite a liking to his star stripper over the years. Sure, he was a crime boss, Don of the something-or-other family, but he was always nice to Dixie. He gave her an amazing job, he tipped her well, and he was very understanding of her struggles with self-control and nymphomania.

When Dixie needed a Sugar Daddy, who better to take care of her?

He offered to make her a kept woman and promised he would take care of paying for whatever her pretty little head could desire. That was real sweet of him, because she could desire so many things. Fortunately, he had proven time and time again that, between his fat wallet and fatter cock, there really was no desire of Dixie's he could not fulfill.

He drafted up a contract, telling Dixie to sell her apartment. Her siblings were skeptical when she said she was getting rid of the place, but according to him, why did she need that apartment when she was going to be kept in a mansion?

Dixie was still unsure of the big commitment he proposed, and she was not alone. The idea of accepting a contract to be the plaything for a shady businessman was a bridge too far for Barbie. "Dixie, this can't be what you want out of life?"

"Why not? I already work for him, and the Boss loves taking care of me. I deserve a life of luxury?"

Barbie folded her arms. "As a sex pet."

"Exactly. You get it."

"I don't!" Barbie groaned in frustration. "Dixie, I know you've accepted this kind of life for yourself, but what you're agreeing to is dangerous. Please, don't be stupid, for once."

Okay, that stung. Dixie was accustomed to being called stupid, but it was always teasing. Even the Boss did it. But Barbie never used it against her like that. She loved Barbie, but maybe their lives were too different.

If Barbie couldn't love her like this, then maybe it was easier being kept than loved. She would focus on the things that still wanted to make her happy: sex, parties, and gifts. Her new owner was happy to give her all three.

After the papers were signed, the Boss grinned, taking them from his giggly new piece of property. Obviously, for legal reasons, that title was nowhere in the text of the document, but with the rights she was handing away, Dixie was his prize to do with as he pleased. He handed the contract to a lawyer, who promptly left the room.

Sure, she was still a little smarter than he preferred when the Silver Queen promised this would happen, but if he wanted a trophy to dangle on his arm, the insatiable blonde would do nicely.

Speaking of insatiable...

"Well, why don't we celebrate?" The Boss slipped the lace blindfold across her eyes, resting comfortably like a mask. He even joked that she had a face suited for masks. "Perfect. Now down on your knees, my pretty birdy..."

Dixie complied, because she knew enough about the papers she signed to know it was her job now to listen to the Boss. The moment she blindly lowered herself to her knees, Dixie was rewarded with the heavy slap of a familiar cock across her cheek. She did not question the term of endearment and what it could mean; the smell of her keeper was emptying her head and all she wanted to do was fill it.

Lucky for her, she had a thick, familiar shaft passing through the "O" she formed with her pillowy lips that would fill that desire quite nicely!

13
Turn a Ho into a Housewife

Dixie enjoyed the lavish lifestyle the Boss offered her, and he clearly enjoyed having her to lounge around the pool and fuck him at his beck and call. Having a live-in stripper meant he had something nice to show off to guests, but it also meant the Boss was dealing with a young party girl whose priorities were, unsurprisingly, wild and independent. He knew what he was signing up when he claimed the impulsive slut for himself, but he knew some pets needed taming. Dixie was no different.

Fortunately, they had a contract to make sure everyone was happy with their arrangement. Even still, he wanted to ease the wild child into the changes he expected to fulfill that contact; it was important to do this right. He could also call in one more favor from the Silver Queen, who seemed entertained enough by his newest proposal to humor him.

Dixie was used to opening gifts from her keeper, but lately, they were moving away from cocktail dresses and micro bikinis. The Boss was still buying her pretty dresses, but now, they were clearly meant to be worn at home with him or when he wanted her to be "presentable" for important company.

It was a style overhaul, but it was important to the Boss—so much so that he made sure to bend her over and take her every time she put on a new polka dotted circle dress to reinforce her good behavior. Dixie was not the brightest bulb, but even she could associate getting her pussy pounded as a reward she wanted to earn again.

As time passed, Dixie was spending less time at the club and more time at special sessions the Boss signed Dixie up for with his nice associate Emily. She was a hypnotherapist who promised to make her better for her owner.

She could not remember what she discussed in those sessions. There was a fancy psychiatry degree on the wall, meaning she could trust the smart hypnotherapist with the silvery hair when she said Dixie did not have to remember their sessions. The important part was how she always left her sessions feeling positive, vibrant, and excited to return home to her man.

Maybe she was just growing up, but the way Dixie made decisions started shifting. She could still make her own decisions; she was her own woman, after all! That said, more often than not, when she made choices, she wanted to make her man happy. And doing what he said always made him happy.

That was her role here, she realized. She was not his "wife," because that was not what she was promised in the contract, but she was his woman. Her role in the house was to support him and listen to his needs whenever she could. When she disobeyed, Dixie knew it upset the Boss, like when she told him she had to visit her family for the weekend. He didn't trust her family, or the rude ex-girlfriend that still hung around with them.

Fortunately, Dixie knew just how to make that up to him! The Boss bought Dixie several fine aprons. As an important man, the Boss had cooks in the Mansion, but she knew he approved when she got in the kitchen herself and whipped up dinner.

She never used to cook, but after her sessions, Dixie was becoming a natural in the kitchen! The Boss joked that women like her belonged in the bedroom and the kitchen, and Dixie was starting to understand what he meant.

When he returned home from a big business meeting, the Boss was greeted by the sight of Dixie in an apron and nothing else. Dixie hoped a warm greeting and the scent of her roast wafting from the oven would help the Boss forgive her for asking to leave.

With a wicked grin, he took her by the shoulder and shoved her down until her tits, barely held in her apron, squished against the countertop. A sharp strike to her exposed ass caused Dixie to jump, only to be held forcefully in place by the Boss's hand. He smacked her two more times, drawing a cry of pleasure from his well-trained pet each time.

Dixie was turned on, but she was still waiting for the Boss to tell her if she was being smacked as a punishment or a reward. She heard the leather of a belt sliding out from a metal buckle, then the loops of the Boss's pants. Hearing the belt buckle hit the floor was enough to make Dixie pant. The Boss's dick was patting the insides of her thighs, and she dutifully shuffled to spread her stance wider for him.

Finally, he leaned over her body and grabbed her throat to pull her close enough to whisper in her ear. His rock-hard length was poking out from between her thighs, sliding against her needy hole with every micromovement. "You were smacked for trying to be selfish and leaving your man." Dixie nodded as best she could in her restrained position. "But you were a good girl trying to make up for your silly mistakes. And good girls get rewarded."

Dixie was drooling, hit by the rush of serotonin that came with earning the Boss's praise. She mewled in appreciation as he repositioned his dick, already wet with her juices, and rammed himself deep in her cunt. Each thrust made her head go fuzzy with bliss, leaving only the most basic and true thoughts to fuel her moans.

Dixie is a good girl.
A good girl always serves her man.
The best reward for a good girl is her man's cock.

14
Knocked-Up Ditzy

Life was a far cry from the vague memories of Dixie as a teenage heroine once upon a time.

Oh, not Dixie. Ditzy! Ditzy kept spacing out, forgetting that the Boss changed her name, paperwork and everything. The longer she lived with Sir, (which was what she was told to call him, but without paperwork,) the more he made decisions for her. Ditzy did not understand much, but she knew that Sir was smart enough to know what was best for her, even when Ditzy forgot.

Sir limited how much time Ditzy was allowed to work out, so her lean muscle was turning to soft flesh that jiggled to the touch. Dancing the pole became a challenge as she fell out of peak shape, so Sir just told her it was time to put dancing aside. It was kind of him to make that choice when she would not.

Sir knows best.

The lack of an outlet for her need to be ogled had Ditzy frustrated and insanely horny, which Sir ~~took advantage of~~ nobly helped his Ditzy work through.

Sir fucked Ditzy daily, and while she thought she had misplaced her birth control like the space cadet she was, in truth, he had confiscated her pills. He said it was her role to give him a child, and the more she thought about it, like with most things, the more she realized Sir was right.

Sir knows best!

Once it was clear Ditzy was pregnant, Sir explained the truth: He knew Ditzy was the same woman who was once the girl hero named Blackwing. That was why he moved her in, claimed her as his, and put his child in her; as a last laugh against her and her mentor for interfering in his business.

Sir knows best?

Ditzy was conflicted, because it would make sense for her to be upset, but nothing had made Sir as happy as she saw him when he explained how she was his slutty, broken hero. That confused Ditzy, because she didn't feel broken. She did feel weak when he roughly bent her over the back of the couch, but that was just because Sir was really strong, and Ditzy was... well, not that anymore.

However she got here, Dixie knew the most important rule: *Sir knows best!* If he tricked her, it was because he was smarter and wanted to make the best choices for her.

After Sir was done claiming her again, Ditzy laid on the plush couch where he left her covered and dripping in his seed, asking if she could tell her adopted father that she was pregnant. She said the news made Sir and Ditzy so happy, and Bryce might be just as happy to be grandfather.

Sir sneered. "That self-righteous fuck won't be meeting any of the brats I'm gonna knock you up with. In fact, you're never seeing any of them again, my dumb little breeder.

That disappointed Ditzy. She wanted to listen to Sir, because that was what her role was in their house, and *Sir knows best,* but she liked her adopted father. And despite their falling out, not seeing Barbie again would make her sad.

Maybe she could tell them about her baby but not that part? Or maybe Sir would realize that Ditzy still wanted to see her family and would respect that! Right?

15
She's Got No Strings (Besides Her Collar and Leash)

The Silver Queen had laid the groundwork for Dixie, now Ditzy, and the Boss to end up together, because her fingerprints were part of the DNA of Ditzy's life at this point. She thought it would be amusing, after he made that dirty comment about her mouth a handful of realities ago, if her fate led her to kneel at his feet as a content, obedient submissive. Much to her pleasure, that was exactly the kind of woman this new Ditzy was.

Unfortunately, the Queen was getting tired of the Boss and his petty vendettas with The Bat. She was not concerned with heroes interfering with her fun, but it would be mildly annoying if a modern retelling of The Trojan War took away the focus from the toy she was graciously **loaning** him.

The Bat was a distraction, but if the Queen made one last adjustment to the timeline, replacing this Ditzy... yes, a new version with a few less strings would let her fun continue uninterrupted.

Sir asked Ditzy to call Bryce and share their good news, but he wanted her to follow it up with the bad news that she was not allowed to talk to him anymore. She wanted to trust Sir, but... well, maybe if she talked to Barbie first. She was a genius.

She was also *very angry*. "He's asking you to cut contact?"

"See, I thought it was weird! But Sir knows best, right?"

"He most certainly does not!" Barbie was still upset, but she remembered what was important. Her voice softened. "Dixie..."

Ditzy winced, like she wasn't supposed to hear that name anymore. But this was Barbie. Somewhere, deep down, her words still held weight. "I know. Barbie, I should have listened to you. I think..."

The crackling sound of static broke her focus. Something was going wrong with her phone. Did the line disconnect? She ended the call and went back to her contact list.

Except... Barbie wasn't in her phone. She scrolled through again, but no luck. She didn't see Bryce's number, either. In fact, there were a few names missing. A few people like... um...

There were people who should have been in her phone. She saw girls from the club and people who were Sirs friends, but weren't some people missing? She was trying so hard to think of the names, but it was like grasping for wisps of smoke. Whatever she wanted to remember was just missing.

She thought maybe she was missing family, but... that was silly; Ditzy had no family. She had a vague memory of a strong male figure of authority in her mind.

It felt like a forever ago, but Dixie grew up on her own, living a quiet life until she started idolizing The Bat. She got it into her head that maybe she could do what he did. Maybe he would take her under his wing!

It was a silly idea. She got beaten by Sir, who showed her how dumb trying to be a hero was. She was disappointed at first, but Sir was confident and smart and knew how the world worked. That was why, when she abandoned her misguided hero worship of The Bat, she learned to admire the man who took her in when she admitted she had nothing to return to in the life she left behind.

From there, Sir was the most important person in her life... right? She was imagining a redhead. Someone freckled and smart and sexy. But everyone knew Ditzy had a thing for redheads. She must have been a passing fancy. Whoever she was, trying to recall her brought a sad smile to Ditzy's pillowy lips.

Soon after taking her in, Sir took Dixie out of college. She was failing anyway, and college never made her happy. Her decisions had a track record of blowing up in her face and ruining everything, but with Sir, she could just... hand her decisions over.

Without a vendetta against The Bat, Sir didn't bother to put Ditzy through playing housewife, and she didn't have the pedigree to be a sugar baby. He didn't even think the name Ditzy was right for her. She was just a dummy who crossed him, and that meant she lost her right to be treated like a person.

Puppy woke up and fastened her collar, which was both a treasured gift and a reminder that good pets behaved. She tried to misbehave once and was disciplined for it. Now that she had signed herself over to him, her one duty was to be a good pet.

And like a good pet, she went to the living room and got to her knees at her designated spot, assuming the position until Sir was ready to tell her what to do.

16
Dumb Doggy

Messing with the timeline was a lot like eating a potato chip; you can't have just one! Dixie, Ditzy, Puppy... whoever she might be, she was just coming along so wonderfully. The Silver Queen was sure one or two more tweaks would leave the ex-vigilante ready for her.

Occasionally, Sir asked Puppy to sign things. They had a contract, but there were always new things Sir was asking for. Today, it was Power of Attorney. Puppy did not know her attorney, so she did not see any issue with signing that away to Sir. He knew what he was doing.

Puppy tried reading the papers Sir gave her, because she was sure she was expected to, but the words were long. Legal words were hard, and between them were shorter words, but those were hard too! There were even numbers in some places.

In fact, the longer she looked at the paper, the more she realized the characters all looked like something vaguely familiar. Things someone tried to teach her once, but she never really understood.

"Hey, you dumb slut. Why are you wasting time?" Sir asked when he checked in and found her still staring at the page. "You pretending to read or something? I'm in a hurry, Puppy. Quit being stupid."

Sir was right; what was she doing? Well, besides staring vacantly at words she couldn't read.

Teachers tried to teach Puppy, she remembered, but she got by as long as she could by cheating and having boys and girls do her homework. By the time she was a teenager, everyone knew she was too dumb to read and Puppy became a high school dropout.

The contract might as well have been in French. For all Puppy knew, it was. At least the words were pretty!

Puppy giggled, crudely writing her name on the line. "Psh, you know I can't quit that, sir!" The Boss rolled his eyes, taking the signed papers.

"Obviously. That's why we changed your name. At least now you only need to know three letters."

"Nu-uh! I know..." She counted the letters in her name. "Six. Wait, five!"

"Puppy, three of those letters are the same."

Blinking in confusion, Puppy looked at the paper again. "Oh gosh, you're right! I'm lucky you're so smart, Sir!"

17
Yes, Sir!

Picking one heroine in the world to play was Emily's best idea in a long time. Something about messing with, retconning, and reshaping Dixie, Ditzy, Puppy, provided her with more entertainment and pleasure than conquering the planet.

But the games couldn't last forever, lest they get stale. It was time to enter the end game, and that meant finally putting an end to the macho crime lord's fun. She was going to throw a wrench in the owner's plans so she could have Puppy to herself.

Puppy did not strip at the club anymore, partially because her arms and legs were too weak to support her on the poles, and partially because Sir didn't want people playing with his pet.

Still, Sir owned the club she used to work at. In the afternoon, he told Puppy that he wanted to attend and would be sending her to the club first to wait for more orders. Puppy complied, as always, feeling particularly agreeable today.

Puppy sat at a table sipping a drink one of the nice girls made her when a man and a woman noticed her from another table. The man called out, "Hey sugartits! Leave that straw alone! Shouldn't lips like those be sucking on my cock instead?"

Blinking, the suggestion sank into Puppy's head. He was right; she had puffy lips like these to suck cock. Sir had literally called them dick sucking lips a few times! When he asked, the way he said it just felt like an absolute truth Puppy could not ignore. Thoughtlessly, she smiled, getting up from her table and walking over.

The man seemed surprised, but when Puppy dropped to her knees, he was not going to question a good thing. When she pawed at the zipper of his jeans, he grabbed her by the arm and led her to an unoccupied backroom.

The moment he released her, Dixie returned to her task, pulling out his dick and wrapping her hand around it, jerking up and down until he quickly got hard for her and she passed his tip past her lips, taking his length into her throat until her glossy lips left an imprint at the base of his cock.

His friend, a woman with short hair dyed blue, asked when she was getting a turn and, as if on instinct, Puppy's mouth rolled back up the man's length, releasing him with a soft pop of her lips. Puppy eagerly pulled down the waistband of a pleasantly surprised punk rock chick. Puppy buried her face between the woman's legs, overcome by the sweet scent of another woman's pussy after so long catering only to—

"Hey bitch, you're not just going to leave me unfinished, right?" the man grumbled, prompting Puppy's hand to work his rod while her tongue delved into the folds of his partner.

The woman smirked, grabbing a fist full of Puppy's blonde hair. "So this is why you come to places like this, then? Just hungry to get fucked? You're just a cum-hungry slut!" The man laughed along as he moved behind Puppy, lifting up her dress just to realize she was already shaking her ass like a happy dog wagging her tail. He shoved his dick deep into her while the bluette wrapped a leg around Puppy's head, pulling her face in closer.

And Puppy loved it all, because she was a cum-hungry slut and this was why she came out tonight!

Through her moans, a thought rattled in her mostly empty head. "Mmm, I think Sir will be here soon," she mumbled, her voice muffled in another woman's crotch.

The man laughed, smacking her ass. The moaning woman grinned, too, purring in Puppy's ear. "Please. A needy bitch like you doesn't need a man. Just something to fuck."

And just like that, Puppy knew she was right. She was here to be fucked, and thoughts of her Sir vanished from her head. She didn't have a man, after all. She did not need a man.

She just needed the bliss that came when the guy behind her groaned and she felt a hot explosion filling her. She cried out in pleasure, and the feverish licking and fingering brought her female fuck partner to climax as well.

When the man was done, he left to clean up in the washroom, leaving Puppy dripping with his cum from one end and drenched in the juices of his friend all over her face.

The friend didn't leave to get cleaned up, though. The blue-haired lady grinned, leaning in close to the soft fuckdoll twitching on the floor. As she bent low to Puppy's ear, the woman's short blue hair grew out, cascading down her shoulders in sleek waves, paling from an ocean blue to a stunning, shiny silver.

18
The Queen's Question

The Silver Queen whispered to Puppy. "You don't need a man. You need your Silver Queen. You were tired of your life of stress and choices and obstacles. I can give that life back to you," she promised.

In that moment, clarity returned like a torrent, hitting Puppy all at once. Not Puppy; Dixie.

There was so much to process, and all of it while sitting on the floor of a strip club, reeking of sex. Dixie not only remembered who she had been, she remembered all the versions of her she had been. The stressed vigilante, the party girl, the stripper, the dolled-up homemaker, and the dumb fuckpet. All of those realities felt exactly that: real. One of them was the first her, but which of them was the real her?

Reading her thoughts, the Silver Queen smiled. "That's your choice. The real you is the one you want to be most; Dixie, Ditzy, or the sweet Puppy." She brushed her thumb across Dixie's lower lip, pulling it back so the Queen's own slickness caught the light before she licked the spot away. "I decide what reality is, and I'm giving the choice to you, darling. What reality would you be happiest with?"

The blonde reflected on her lives. It was an easy choice, right? She was a hero once. There was a version of her that people respected and admired, who was strong and smart and made the world better.

That was the version of her racked with stress, constantly shouldering the weight of the world. She was a hero overworking herself because she was so scared to fail, the moment she was released from her burdens, she spiraled in the other direction. That wasn't the Silver Queen, she knew deep down; Dixie was so tightly wound by her responsibilities, that when she was free of them, she jumped on every reckless, impulsive decision that would only hurt her.

Ditzy thought to the other iterations of her, giving each thought as the world around her felt still, like time was waiting for her to make a choice. Puppy thought, finally, about the reality that led her to this very spot, cum-soaked and following commands like a trained bitch in heat. She wanted to call herself useless, but she wasn't.

Taking commands from anyone who passed by had been too far. Thinking of all the ways that could have gone wrong terrified and stressed her out. And it had been so long since she felt stress like that, Puppy could feel her stomach turn.

When she was Sir's... the Boss's obedient pet, things were easy. She didn't trust the Boss with the hindsight of all her lives, but she felt satisfied handing her leash, figuratively and literally, to someone who would spoil her and let her live a life of simple, slutty service.

"...if I... um..."

"Don't be shy, Puppy," the Queen cooed, knowing the name the ex-vigilante had picked for herself in her own head.

"If I go back to being a pet—"

"An empty-headed, obedient, attention-loving slut of a pet," the Queen clarified, wanting Puppy to acknowledge every aspect of who she wanted to become.

Puppy shuddered as a wave of intense arousal hit her with each word the Queen uttered. Meekly, she nodded. "If that's the me I want to be... do I have to go back to the Boss?"

The Silver Queen grinned from ear to ear. She could have done so many things differently. She could have just remade Dixie to be the exact Puppy kneeling in a puddle of sex begging to submit to her completely.

But how much more delicious was it to give Puppy all the tools to come to the choice on her own? Well, with some well-intentioned help along the way. "Never. In fact, I'm sure that man will have his own change of fortune in the near future. He won't be needing to concern himself with pet care."

Puppy opened her mouth, but Dixie cut in before she could sign her rights away again. She had an easy, carefree life in front of her, but she couldn't shake one thing: Barbie. She put Barbie through so much, and that was all while she was still Dixie. Leaving Barbie alone was the kind thing to do.

But she still loved Barbie. She gave her up once, and she didn't want to do it again. "I know, deep down, that being your puppy is where I belong. But I don't want to give up Barbie," she pleaded.

That was a wrinkle in The Queen's otherwise perfect plan. This bimbo hero still found ways to amuse her. "Reality is my plaything, dear. I can make it work."

Puppy smiled, looking up at the stunning villainess with pleading, puppy dog eyes. "You promise?"

That was all the confirmation she needed. The Queen held out her hand, letting a silvery leash form from nothing, leading itself to the collar Puppy already wore securely around her neck. "I'll make sure you're taken good care of, precious pet."

A content smile crossed Puppy's face as awareness faded from her crystal blue eyes. Unnecessary memories and IQ points drained away, belonging to different women who never existed. Thoughts and concerns drifted into oblivion until the Silver Queen looked down and all that was left was the real Puppy; *her* Puppy looking up with wide eyes and a dopey look, waiting for her owner to make decisions for her.

"I think it's time to finally take you home," the Queen decided. "I have someone for you to meet."

"Yay!" Puppy wiggled in place on her knees, excited to go with her master, exactly like a good pet would.

Oh, she couldn't resist. "Puppy, bark for your queen."

"Arf!"

"Good girl."

Epilogue
Her Sweet Princess

The Silver Queen stirred in the plush King-sized bed in her mansion. There was a figure, curled up and naked, resting near her feet on the bed. The Queen was accustomed to bringing in a warm body to fill her bed and her holes when the mood struck her, but she had never been a pet owner before.

She expected she might get tired of her new possession eventually, but the dumb, obedient little puppy was a welcome addition to her home routine. And if Emily ever got too bored, she had someone else to take care of her.

The never-a-heroine's name was not Puppy anymore, even if that was what she was. The Boss was a simple brute, and Emily was happy to rewrite his destiny to stick him as the thankless bouncer for the club he owned in another life.

The Queen wanted to give her pet an appropriate name. What better than to make her into the Queen's little Princess. Okay, so her full name was Princess Pussylicker, but that was a mouthful to use in everyday conversation. Handling mouthfuls was more within her fuckpup's skillset anyway.

Sitting up and letting the silk sheets slide off her perfectly perky breasts, the Queen patted the spot next to her on the bed to get Princess' attention. The pet blinked awake with a foggy awareness of where she was. It was understandable; some animals were too dumb to remember things easily.

When she realized she was being beckoned by her master, Princess scrambled to the spot. She sat on her knees right where her Queen wanted her. "Morning, my Queen!" She was human in species and an animal in rank, but the Queen let her start her days allowed to speak until commanded otherwise.

The Silver Queen smiled, grabbing a handful of her pet's heavy tit. They were a source of endless fun, to the point where she woke up some days considering an addition to Princess and her sexed-up body. Ultimately, she decided her pet was perfect. If she wanted an ex-heroine with tits the size of beachballs, she could keep that in mind for next time.

Looking at Princess, with her dopey grin and need to please, the Queen was sure this would be more than a one-time indulgence. When you unmade a vigilante and turned her into something so much better, how could you resist the urge to begin a collection? The reality-bender finally had an outlet for her boredom and a world full of heroes and heroines she could play with. The possibilities were endless.

"Good morning, slut. Are you hungry?" The pup nodded. "Hungry for your Queen?" The nodding hastened. All these months later and her Princess was still insatiable.

The Queen ran a finger up her slit, transforming herself. It was a common part of their morning routine to have Princess lap her up for breakfast, but the Queen was in a different mood, and it called for an adjustment in the form of a long, thick shaft growing between the Queen's legs, just below her carefully manicured tuft of silver hair.

Princess drooled at the sight of her Master's cock. She was always drooling these days; it all came down to whether it was an absentminded drool or a hungry drool. The way Princess' neck was already craning low to get closer to eye-level with the tip of her dick made it clear she was craving her Queen.

The monarch obliged her, grabbing her blonde hair and dragging her dick suckers over to wrap around her. "Mmm, good girl. After we feed you today, I have important plans." Soft hums of pleasure slipped between her words. Her Princess had grown to be quite the expert with her tongue, wrapping around the Queen's cock as she took her length deep into her throat.

Princess wanted to respond, but she was, quite frankly, dumb enough to forget that talking with a throat full of Queendick was impossible. The vibrations did push the Queen closer to the edge, at least. "Silly little slut. You want to know what I have planned? Well, I have this well-trained beauty of a bitch I own, so what kind of Master would I be if I wasted a perfect opportunity to breed her?"

The Queen repositioned her knee so her Princess could settle herself between the long legs of her superior. Brushing shiny blonde hair away from Princess' face, the Queen regained her composure after an unexpected moan. "Does that make you wet with excitement, Princess? Knowing Master's going to give you the gift of her cock to pump that cunt of yours? To fill you to bursting with my cum until you're a knocked-up pup?"

The twinkle of pure excitement in her Princess' eyes answered the question better than any attempt at gagged words. She wanted nothing more than to be fucked by her Queen until she could be her breeding vessel. The blind, obedient loyalty of her tamed bimbo pet finished the Silver Queen. Her own mind went deliciously blank as her body shook with the throes of an orgasm.

Hot jets of silvery-white cum coated Princess' throat and filled all the space left between her cheeks and tongue. The pet sputtered until there was no room left and semen forced its way out of the otherwise airtight seal her swollen lips formed around a cock.

The Queen unsheathed her dick from Princess' throat, resting the cum-coated member on her cheek. Even with excess batter leaking from not just her mouth but her nose, Princess beamed, rubbing her face against her favorite cock. "You like that, you little cum-drunk animal?"

Princess cooed, licking the sides of the Queen's dick clean like it was her privilege to cater to the manifested cock. "Hehe, *your* animal," she whispered, proud of her place with the Queen, even if that place was begging at her feet. "Master's so nice, feeding Princess so well."

The Silver Queen sat up, grabbing her Princess' sticky cheek to claim a salty sweet kiss from her puppygirl. "A good girl knows her place," she affirmed, rewarding the undone vigilante's good behavior. She had come so far. "And there's so much of your Queen's cum in your future, you lucky girl."

And Princess really did feel lucky. Luckier than some silly what's-her-name that never was. The Queen promised her a perfect, happy life, and she delivered.

"Are you playing with Princess *already*?"

Princess' attention snapped to the bedroom door, where a beautiful redhead entered in her nightie. She didn't remember it, but this was the other part of Princess' request.

Barbie was brilliant prodigy, plucked from her first year at university to become the Queen's personal protégé. The offer was too alluring to ignore, and Barbie gave up life as The Bat's sidekick to serve as her personal assistant, running the day-to-day operations of Emily's companies.

And from the moment The Queen brought Barbie home, Princess was in love. And Barbie adored Princess in return! There was no more need for the on-again, off-again drama. The girls could be happy together in the palm of their Queen's hand.

"I hope I'm not intruding, Ma'am?" Her eyes were already glued to Princess' perfect body.

The reality-bender chuckled, giving Princess a smack on the ass to signal that she was allowed to greet Barbie. Even after all the manipulation, those two still shared something unique, and The Queen didn't have to feel jealous, because she owned them both.

Princess wasted no time, peppering the redhead with cum-flavored kisses the moment she knelt to meet her. It wasn't the first time Barbie tasted the Queen's seed, obviously.

"I was just letting our sweet pet know that she we're going to breed her soon."

Barbie ran her fingers into Princess' hair, petting her. "Lucky girl! Can I help, Ma'am?" She couldn't breed the petgirl, but she would still be an enthusiastic participant.

The Silver Queen mulled it over, playing it up as two sets of pathetic eyes begged her to reward them. Those two really were damn cute sometimes. "Oh, fine. Her mouth will need something to do, anyway."

The girls cheered, racing to climb onto The Queen's massive bed. Princess had a full morning with her Owner, the Queen, pumping behind her and her lover, Barbie, splayed out before her. What life could be better than this?

Don't miss out!

Visit the website below and you can sign up to receive emails whenever Layla Rose publishes a new book. There's no charge and no obligation.

https://books2read.com/r/B-A-PBIWE-EZGSB

BOOKS 2 READ

Connecting independent readers to independent writers.

Did you love *Bimbofication of a Vigilante: Blackwing*? Then you should read *Build-a-Bimbo Heroine: Miracle Girl*[1] by Layla Rose!

The Silver Queen, a reality-bending villainess, listlessly longs for something to do with her immense powers that won't bore her to death.

Watching the tantalizing heroines of the world running around with their idealism, morals, and modest talents, she decides there are no better toys to play with. But wouldn't it be better to build a toy from scratch before breaking it?

---

1. https://books2read.com/u/3LnDBD

2. https://books2read.com/u/3LnDBD

Jeanie Gray is an unassuming reporter, or at least she was. After waking up one day with unexplained superpowers, she took the miracle as a sign to become a heroine. Her career was off to an exciting start when suddenly, her Miracles became... different.

Powers evolve, but with her body, libido, and mind developing in lewd ways, Miracle Girl has to learn how her new, slutty Miracles can serve her purpose as a heroine.

Read more at https://www.tumblr.com/cottonundiestf.

Also by Layla Rose

The Silver Queen's Superharem
Bimbofication of a Vigilante: Blackwing
Build-a-Bimbo Heroine: Miracle Girl
A Super Bimbofication: Superiorgirl

Watch for more at https://www.tumblr.com/cottonundiestf.

About the Author

Layla is a trans woman who has a thing for erotic transformations, bimbofication, and any story that can change someone into something sillier, sexier, and sometimes, stranger.

Some of her stories started as "Suggestion Series," where she offered up a heroine and had her readers anonymously suggest ways she should be transformed.

If you enjoy Layla's lewd content, or want to join her comfy community, be sure to join her Discord!

Thank you to DarkMoney1 for the Layla art!

Read more at https://linktr.ee/cottonundies.